Dear Parents:

Congratulations! Your child is taking the first steps on an exciting journey. The destination? Independent reading!

STEP INTO READING® will help your child get there. The program offers five steps to reading success. Each step includes fun stories and colorful art or photographs. In addition to original fiction and books with favorite characters, there are Step into Reading Non-Fiction Readers, Phonics Readers and Boxed Sets, Sticker Readers, and Comic Readers—a complete literacy program with something to interest every child.

Learning to Read, Step by Step!

Ready to Read   Preschool–Kindergarten
• big type and easy words • rhyme and rhythm • picture clues
For children who know the alphabet and are eager to begin reading.

Reading with Help   Preschool–Grade 1
• basic vocabulary • short sentences • simple stories
For children who recognize familiar words and sound out new words with help.

Reading on Your Own   Grades 1–3
• engaging characters • easy-to-follow plots • popular topics
For children who are ready to read on their own.

Reading Paragraphs   Grades 2–3
• challenging vocabulary • short paragraphs • exciting stories
For newly independent readers who read simple sentences with confidence.

Ready for Chapters   Grades 2–4
• chapters • longer paragraphs • full-color art
For children who want to take the plunge into chapter books but still like colorful pictures.

STEP INTO READING® is designed to give every child a successful reading experience. The grade levels are only guides; children will progress through the steps at their own speed, developing confidence in their reading.

Remember, a lifetime love of reading starts with a single step!

Visit us on the Web!
StepIntoReading.com
randomhousekids.com

Educators and librarians, for a variety of teaching tools, visit us at RHTeachersLibrarians.com

ISBN 978-1-5247-6801-0 (trade) — ISBN 978-1-5247-6802-7 (lib. bdg.)

Printed in the United States of America

10 9 8 7 6 5 4 3 2 1

nickelodeon

FAR-OUT FRIENDS!

by Delphine Finnegan

based on the teleplay
"Rusty's Space Bit" by Elize Morgan

illustrated by Dave Aikins

Random House 🏠 New York

Whee!
Botasaur gives
the Bits a bounce.

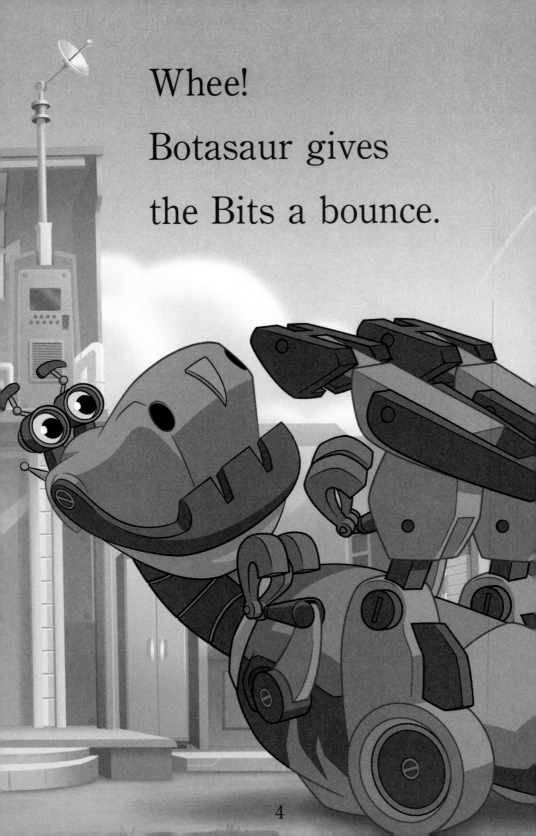

Ray, Whirly, Crush, and Jack fly into the sky.

Rusty is
in the air, too!

They all land safely.

But what is still

up in the sky?

It lands close by.
Rusty and Ruby
and the Bits
check it out.

Ruby scans it.

It is Orbit.

He is from outer space!

He is far from home.

Can Rusty and Ruby help
Orbit get back home?

The friends come up
with an idea!

Rusty turns up
Botasaur's power.
He will send Orbit
home with a big kick.

But now Orbit is missing—
and so is Jack!

Whew!

Orbit and Jack are

at the playground.

Rusty and Ruby tell Orbit,
"We can get you home!"
Jack does not want
Orbit to leave.

Botasaur launches Orbit. But Orbit flies the wrong way.

Next they try
a jet pack.
It loses power.

Jack makes a house for Orbit.

He wants his friend to stay.

But Orbit must go home.

Rusty and Ruby
build a shuttle.
Ruby has another surprise.
She has put a camera on Orbit!

Now Jack can keep in touch with his far-out friend! Goodbye, Orbit! Thanks for visiting!